Jane Clarke & Britta Teckentrup

NEON LEON

nosy crow™

An imprint of Candlewick Press

Leon is a chameleon.
He's in this picture.
Which chameleon do you think is Leon?

Chameleons can change color
to **match** their surroundings.

Where do you think the chameleons are going?
Let's turn the page
and find out.

The chameleons are in a leafy jungle.
And they've all turned **green!** They **match!**
They're hard to spot, aren't they?

Well, all except for Leon.
He's still **orange**.

What do you think will happen when the chameleons go to a **sandy** desert?

Yes! They **match.**
The chameleons have
all turned **yellow!**

Well, all except for Leon.
He's still **orange!**

Hmm . . . let's see if Leon can do any
better in the big, **gray**, rocky mountains.
Can you help him this time? Tell Leon
what color he should turn.

I don't think he can hear you.
Can you say it **louder**?

All the chameleons are hidden among the rocks.
They **match** . . . but has Leon changed color?
No, he's still **very orange.** Poor Leon.

Maybe he'll feel better after a good
night's sleep back in the jungle.
Let's say, "Good night, Leon," and softly turn the page.

Oh, dear. Leon's so **bright,** he's keeping
all the other chameleons awake!
What a **lot** of grumpy chameleons!

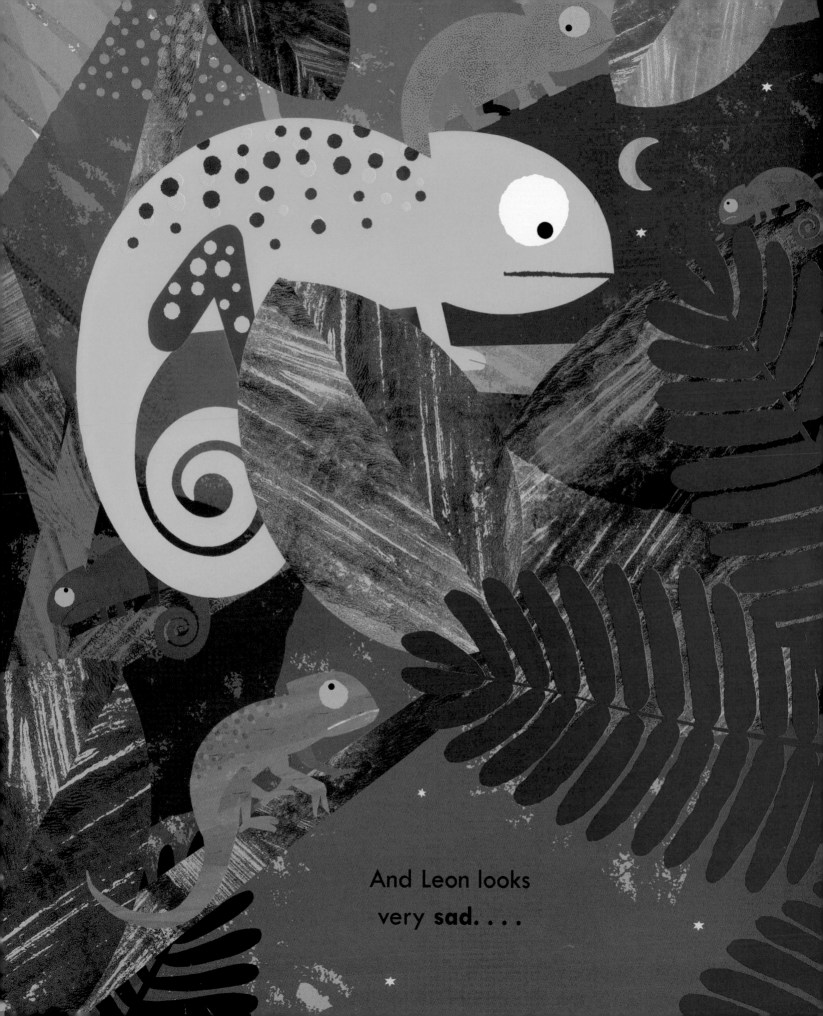

And Leon looks
very **sad**. . . .

Where's Leon going now?
Do you think he's looking for
somewhere he can fit in?

Look! He's found the perfect place already.
Everyone here is **orange,** just like Leon!

He matches!

But, oh no! The birds are flying
up, up, up into the bright **blue** sky.
Maybe they've gone to find
something to eat.

And now Leon doesn't fit in anymore.

Whisper, "Don't worry, Leon.
Everything will be okay."

But what's that over there in
the corner of the page?
Could it be something . . .

orange?

Hurry, Leon!

But Leon can't walk very fast, can he?
We'd better give him a bit of time.
Let's count to **ten**, then turn the page. . . .

At last, Leon's found a place he can fit in!
All the flowers are **orange.**

And look! Leon's **happy.**

Let's all clap our hands and
smile, smile, smile with him.

But there's one thing that would make Leon
even **happier.** Can you guess what that is?

That's right! Leon's found a **friend.**
Can you spot them both?

It's the perfect match.

To Angelina and
Sammy — J. C.

For Sanja — B. T.

Nosy Crow and its logos are trademarks of Nosy Crow Ltd.
Used under license.

First U.S. edition 2018

Library of Congress Catalog Card Number pending
ISBN 978-0-7636-9915-4

18 19 20 21 22 23 WKT 10 9 8 7 6 5 4 3 2 1

Printed in Shenzhen, Guangdong, China

This book was typeset in Tw Cen MT.
The illustrations were created digitally.

Nosy Crow
an imprint of
Candlewick Press
99 Dover Street
Somerville, Massachusetts 02144

www.nosycrow.com
www.candlewick.com